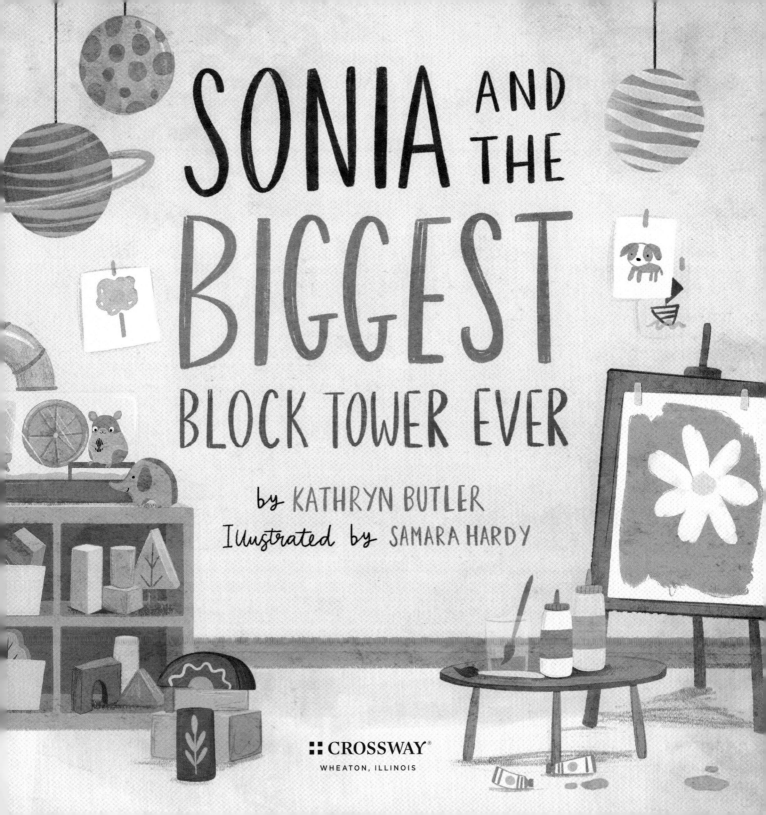

SONIA AND THE BIGGEST BLOCK TOWER EVER

by KATHRYN BUTLER

Illustrated by SAMARA HARDY

CROSSWAY®

WHEATON, ILLINOIS

Sonia and the Biggest Block Tower Ever

© 2025 by Kathryn Butler

Illustrations © 2025 by Crossway

Published by Crossway
1300 Crescent Street
Wheaton, Illinois 60187

Published in association with the literary agency of Wolgemuth & Wilson.

Illustrations, book design, and cover design: Samara Hardy

First printing 2025

Printed in China

ISBN: 978-1-4335-9809-8

Library of Congress Cataloging-in-Publication Data

Names: Butler, Kathryn L., 1980– author. | Hardy, Samara, illustrator.

Title: Sonia and the biggest block tower ever / by Kathryn Butler ; illustrated by Samara Hardy.

Description: Wheaton, Illinois : Crossway, 2025. | Audience term: Children | Audience: Ages 3–7.

Identifiers: LCCN 2024016180 | ISBN 9781433598098 (hardcover)

Subjects: CYAC: Self-esteem—Fiction. | Blocks (Toys)—Fiction. | Christian life—Fiction. | LCGFT: Christian fiction. | Picture books.

Classification: LCC PZ7.1.B8935 So 2025 | DDC [E]—dc23

LC record available at https://lccn.loc.gov/2024016180

Crossway is a publishing ministry of Good News Publishers.

RRDS			34	33	32	31	30	29	28	27	26	25
15	14	13	12	11	10	9	8	7	6	5	4	3	2	1

"He will rejoice over you with gladness;

he will quiet you by his love;

he will exult over you with loud singing."

ZEPHANIAH 3:17

"Wonderful, all of you!" Mrs. Kim told the kids during playtime.

Kevin and Rosa were painting pictures of daisies that seemed to bloom off the pages. Isabel wove a pretty bracelet with purple and green thread, and Tiago told Mrs. Kim all about his glass jar that had leaves and a wriggling woolly bear caterpillar inside.

But Sonia crossed her arms and plopped on the playroom carpet.

How am I wonderful? Sonia asked herself with a frown. *I don't paint or make bracelets or catch caterpillars. No one thinks what I do is special.* She leaned her chin on her hand, stacked a few blocks into a tower, and imagined a caterpillar weaving bracelets from flower petals and fine silk. If she had one of *those*, Mrs. Kim would say she was wonderful.

"You've started a beautiful block tower, Sonia!" Mrs. Kim said. "You have a real talent for building."

"I do?" Mrs. Kim's words felt like warm sunshine to Sonia. As Mrs. Kim walked away, Sonia thought maybe she *could* be wonderful. *What if I build a BIG tower? The biggest ever? Then people will know I'm special! I can see it now . . .*

The classroom and the kids and talk of caterpillars faded away as Sonia pictured how glorious it would be to make the biggest block tower ever.

Sonia imagined that she began by scooping up a few wooden blocks from the shelf and stacking them—one, two, three, four, five—until they rose to double the size of her little tower.

Mrs. Kim clapped her hands. "Very nice, Sonia!" Sonia looked around. She wanted the kids to clap, too. *I'll make it even bigger! Then they'll know I'm special.*

Next, Sonia scooped all the wooden blocks from the shelf in a big bundle. She piled them—six, seven, eight, nine, ten . . . so many that she lost count. Sonia climbed on top of a chair to add the last blocks. "Ta-da!"

Rosa giggled and Isabel flashed a smile. "Well done, Sonia!" Mrs. Kim said.

Sonia spun around and searched the classroom. She wanted *more* smiles and nice words. "Just watch! I'll make it even taller!" she said. She grabbed some books from the shelf and stacked them on top.

The tower had to be even higher! She grabbed a fire truck, a checkers game, and six boxes of crayons.

Tiago gave Sonia a thumbs-up, and she felt giddy with excitement. But it wasn't enough. She wanted *more. It has to be higher!* she thought.

Sonia dashed around the room like a tiny tornado, scooping up marker bins, craft dough, and a bucket of pipe cleaners.

She grabbed Mrs. Kim's plastic food and boxes of costumes, rolls of stickers, and cartons of glue.

As the stack piled toward the ceiling, Sonia raced up to the top and then down, up and then down again. She stretched and reached and strained to build her tower higher and higher.

Finally, she wedged the cage of Honeybun, Mrs. Kim's golden hamster, at the very top. Then, with a final push, the cage poked a hole in the ceiling with a *pop*! Sunlight spilled through.

The children all gathered in the beam of sunlight and cheered. Mrs. Kim dabbed her eyes with a tissue. All the other teachers in the school flocked to the classroom to see Sonia's tower. "It's amazing!" they cried. "She's wonderful!"

Sonia's heart raced. *It has to be higher!* She rushed to snatch every lunchbox and backpack from the cubbies.

She hauled up the globe, the trash bin, and armfuls of stuffed animals and puppets.

She hauled up the desk, the blackboard, the art cabinet, and the play oven. Then, with a mighty tug, she tore the drinking fountain off the wall and hauled it up, too.

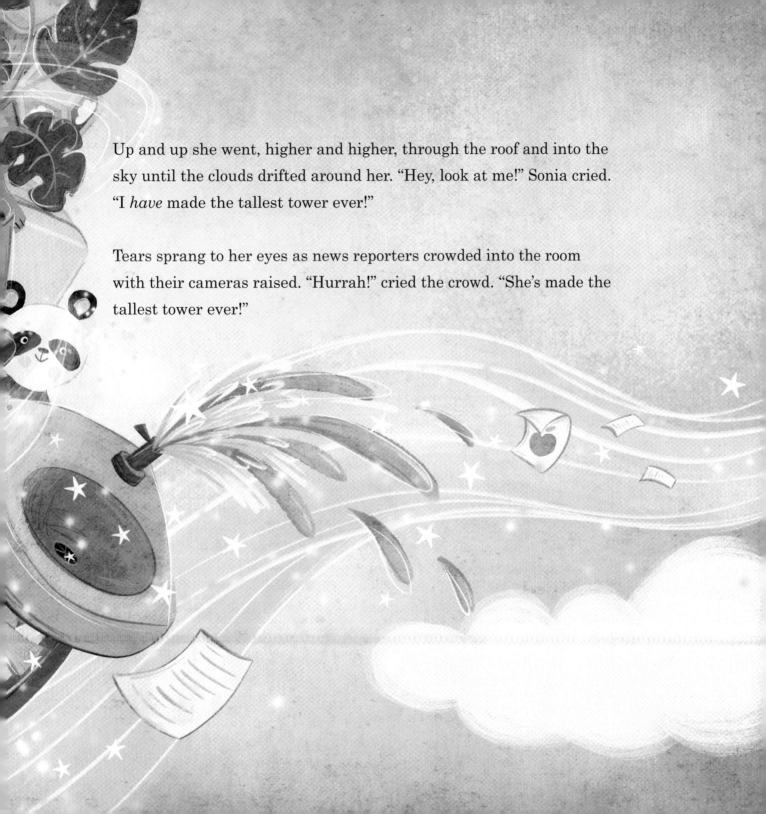

Up and up she went, higher and higher, through the roof and into the sky until the clouds drifted around her. "Hey, look at me!" Sonia cried. "I *have* made the tallest tower ever!"

Tears sprang to her eyes as news reporters crowded into the room with their cameras raised. "Hurrah!" cried the crowd. "She's made the tallest tower ever!"

"Sonia? Are you okay?"

The sound of Mrs. Kim's voice startled Sonia. She blinked and looked around uneasily. It was so silent. She glanced down, and although she could still see the crowd cheering wildly, she couldn't hear their applause anymore. They were so far, far below.

They were very far below.

"Wow, it sure is a long way down," Sonia said, wrapping her arms around a jumble of stuffed animals.

Whoosh. An airplane rushed past, and Sonia's tower wobbled in the breeze. Suddenly, Sonia felt scared and alone. A bluebird sang to cheer her, but when it landed on the topmost lunchbox,

the tower swayed left—

and then it swayed right—

and then finally . . .

Crash! Sonia's tower tumbled down, down to the ground. Boxes banged and clanged. Honeybun squeaked. Sonia sailed through the air, fell through the roof, and landed *sploosh* into a pile of sock puppets.

Sonia sat up, blinked, and looked around. No sock puppets or blocks. No news reporters or cheering kids. And Honeybun was safe in his cage.

Just ten blocks lay toppled across the floor. And all the applause she'd loved had fallen silent.

Sonia started to cry. It would never work! She couldn't build the biggest block tower after all. She'd *never* be special.

"Sonia, what's the matter?" Mrs. Kim asked.

"I wanted to build the biggest block tower ever so that everyone would think I'm special," Sonia said. "But I can't! I'll never be special."

Mrs. Kim dried Sonia's face with her shirtsleeve. "Sonia, whatever do you mean? You *are* special—very special! But that's not because of what you can build. And it's not because of any nice words people might say about you."

Sonia blinked away her tears. "What do you mean?" she asked.

"You're special because God made you in his image, to reflect his goodness. You don't have to build the tallest tower for him to notice you or love you. God knows you're special, so it doesn't matter what other people think about you."

That's right, God does love me! The thought flooded over Sonia like the warmest sunshine. Her heart started to race again, even more than it had when Mrs. Kim had clapped for her. She broke into a smile.

She knew now that someone was always cheering for her. She hadn't built a tower that reached the sky, or even an itty-bitty one with ten blocks. Yet someone was clapping—someone wonderful—someone who'd built the tallest mountains. Someone who had died for her sins. He was clapping and clapping, and he loved her.

Sonia glanced at the blocks scattered on the floor, scooped them up, and tucked them back on the shelf. Then she walked over to see her friends.

Kevin and Rosa taught her how to paint flowers. Isabel showed her how to weave bracelets. And Tiago told her everything he knew about caterpillars.

Sonia listened with a wide grin on her face, and she clapped and clapped for each and every one.

Before she went home, Sonia built one last tower with just five blocks, enough to showcase Isabel's bracelets (or to give Tiago's caterpillar a fun place to climb). As she stacked the last block, she remembered how much God loved her.

Then she went out into the sunshine, thanking God for blocks and friends and hands that build.

THE END

Note to Kids

HAVE YOU EVER FELT LIKE SONIA? Have you ever thought that if you could do things just a bit bigger or just a bit better, you could make people like you?

The good news is that no matter what you do, and no matter what others think of you, God loves you! He made you in his image, and in his sight you are wonderful and precious (Gen. 1:27; Ps. 139:14). He loves you so much that he gave his one and only Son for you (John 3:16). The favor of others doesn't matter when we have God's love. He cares that we love him and our neighbors (Matt. 22:37–39) so much more than he cares about the height of our tallest block towers.